Frosty Windows

FROSTY WINDOWS

DAVID GEBHART

iUniverse, Inc.
Bloomington

Frosty Windows

iUniverse books may be ordered through booksellers or by contacting:

iUniverse
1663 Liberty Drive
Bloomington, IN 47403
www.iuniverse.com
1-800-Authors (1-800-288-4677)

ISBN: 978-1-4759-7451-5 (sc)
ISBN: 978-1-4759-7452-2 (ebk)

Library of Congress Control Number: 2013901964

Printed in the United States of America

iUniverse rev. date: 02/19/2013

CHAPTER 1

There are rare times in history when men and women of genius and vision combine great wisdom and knowledge of the distant past and make extraordinary use of it in the present, hoping to influence the future. This was true of two nineteenth-century physicians, a father and son.

They were convinced after much research and travel that the Japanese and Chinese, like their ancestors, understood the relationship between human chemistry and electrical transmission in the body. They also evaluated how stress impacts the cells, tissues, and organ systems. Just as important, they learned firsthand and through research in Japanese and Chinese healing literature. They did extensive research into the impacts of poor nutrition and explored how specific foods and natural compounds can be used for treatment and prevention of degenerative diseases.

This approach to medicine was totally rejected by the Medical Society of London. Exploring the actual causes of disease, as the ancient Japanese and Chinese healers did, was beyond the scope of contemporary medical practices. The British and the Europeans concentrated on treating symptoms of disease. John and Evan Lunt, both MDs, were so intent in the pursuit of scientific truth that they were oblivious to the medical world around them. They developed a thriving practice in London. They had the loyalty and admiration of many thankful patients. However, the Medical Society of London didn't appreciate their practicing Oriental medicine. They were not welcome in medical society, and their peers continually ridiculed them.

"It is obvious that ignorance and fear have won again," John said.

"Yes, John, and don't forget their paranoia concerning their loss of power and recognition. Also, the prospect of losing revenue is a real threat to them," his father replied.

John exclaimed bitterly, "I can't believe we have been asked to stop practicing medicine that is not acceptable to the Medical Society of London or face losing the legal right to practice at all."

John and his dad felt they had no choice and began preparing to leave London and start over in America. Both doctors had visited Boston several times. The shipping company they owned consisted of twelve fast cargo ships. John's grandfather had left this company to them. The company, based in Boston, often traded with Japan and China. They had friends in Boston and many times had sailed to Japan and China from there in pursuit of knowledge of the Oriental approach to healing. Still, both men felt betrayed and insulted. After all, they were board-certified physicians.

"How can men of science be so blind? We have cured patients that they gave up on."

"John, I think that is a big part of our problem. It is our success that is getting to them."

"I suppose you are right, Dad. But we offered to explain our Japanese treatment and prevention systems to them. Remember? We even demonstrated the effects of specific compounds and how they worked to accelerate the healing process with one of our own patients. They rejected it, called it . . . What was that? Spontaneous remission! Well, I suppose we have to get on with this packing. Look at this," he said, handing his father a photograph. "It is Carolyn just before she contracted typhoid fever. She was so beautiful. I loved her so. She would have been so proud of our work.

If only she wouldn't have insisted on helping those unfortunate poor kids down on the waterfront. I lost her to it—that terrible typhoid fever that started on the waterfront."

"It was an epidemic, Son. Many of our patients and friends died too. All of London suffered."

"If I get another chance at real love, I will do everything in my power to protect it. I just won't let her be exposed to danger."

"John, you have been in a black mood now for two years. I know it's been difficult. As you know, I have been through it also. I did everything I could, but your mother died of lung cancer anyway. John, I learned you can't live in the past. My faith in God pulled me through. God will do the same for you. Just trust Him."

"Yes, Father. Thank God I trusted Him as my savior this last summer."

The two doctors decided to relocate to the Boston area. During the first two months of living there they met many people such as pastors, professionals, lawyers, judges, hardworking laborers, many sailors and ship captains. Also, they took time to meet some physicians. John and his dad seemed to be accepted, even liked. One day in the fall, they traveled south of Boston about twelve miles. The road was rocky and rutted and seemed to gradually climb. The horse pulling their rig seemed to strain a bit. Finally, they spotted a huge mansion on the edge of a forest of tall, old oaks, situated near cliffs overlooking the ocean. As they came closer, it became obvious that the mansion was abandoned.

They found that the house had belonged to a merchant who'd died in an accident. He had been elderly and had no living relatives. The house was scheduled to go up for auction soon.

At the auction, the two doctors had no trouble winning the bid. It had thirty-five rooms, with a large ballroom, four sitting rooms, and fourteen bedrooms with four balconies. It was within three hundred feet of the cliffs overlooking the ocean. The oaks were close by.

The house was to be a day clinic. However, it was remodeled to accommodate patients who needed to be observed for a night or longer. They hired five full-time physicians who had practices but were intrigued with the progressive way the two doctors practiced medicine and wanted to learn all they could. They were well paid. John also handpicked five experienced nurses.

At first everything seemed to go well. Word spread quickly that people were getting great treatment and being healed. Some local physicians were intrigued and referred their difficult cases to them. There were the usual naysayers, who tried to protect their own practices by speaking out against the clinic. Somehow it never occurred to John and his dad that resentment was building.

The two obviously didn't need the revenue generated from practicing their brand of medicine. Their shipping business more than paid for the expenses of the practice. After a year, John and Evan were very popular with many people in and near Boston. Their patients were getting well for the most part; however, the chief of staff at Boston General Hospital, Dr. Crill, was very upset with them, even though John and his dad were careful to send some seriously ill patients to the hospital for intensive treatment. They visited these patients regularly and sometimes suggested remedies that were not on the hospital formulary.

John and his father did not notice the extent of this resentment. After one long and strenuous day, an unexpected visitor came to their clinic. It was Dr. Crill. He was directed to one of the lounges, where John and Evan were resting.

"Well, Dr. Crill, what brings you to our humble establishment?"

Crill began to turn red. Looking straight into John's eyes, in a low, almost whisper, he said, "You know, Doctor, Boston General has one of the finest staffs in American medicine. Frankly, we do not appreciate you and your father imposing this Japanese medicine on our citizens!"

"Well, Dr. Crill, I'm sorry you feel that way. Are you upset because our patients are improving at a pace rarely seen with your standard medicine at the hospital?"

In nearly a rage Crill stated, "We are watching you two. Just stay out of our way."

Crill turned on his heels, brushing aside one of the doctors coming into the lounge. He seemed to be muttering to himself.

"What was that all about, John?"

"It's London all over again, Father. Let's get out of here tonight; there is a world-renowned soloist appearing at the Palace." This was an easy choice. John loved the theater, opera, and great singing. John and his dad were not disappointed. Louise Morrell, the featured singer, was an exceptionally talented soprano with magnificent range. She was also very beautiful—tall, with flaming red hair and large dark eyes that flashed like lightning when she sang her arias.

All of these attributes did not go unnoticed by John, who was six foot one, broad shouldered, handsome, and well built. He had thick, wavy black hair. He also had an elegant but modest manner about him. His dad was about five foot eight, stocky, and in good shape physically, with a quick wit and a pleasant personality.

Both men believed that being physically fit was a necessity because of their constant exposure to sickness, and they wanted to serve as good examples for their patients. John and his father became regular patrons of Miss Morrell's concerts. John always sat as close to the stage as possible when Louise performed. One night early in her performance, their eyes met. John wasn't sure, but he thought she'd noticed him. *She definitely noticed me,* he thought. He was sure she'd smiled his way. He could not contain himself. He had to meet her. This time he made his way to her dressing room. He was met by a very large, dark-complexioned man who seemed to be standing vigil at the door.

"Monsieur, what is it that you want?"

John was not sure what to say. He smiled and said that he was Doctor Lunt and wished to see Miss Morrell. The large man by the door looked concerned.

"She is not well, Doctor?" he said in a low but polite voice. John thought that he would get in to see her only by using a slight deception. He had a card. On the front of it, he quickly wrote, "I must see you." He handed the card to the man, who smiled and about-faced. Still smiling, but with a sense of urgency, the man entered her dressing room. It took ten long minutes, but he returned.

"You must only take five minutes; follow me."

John was elated. He felt like a schoolboy meeting his first young girl.

She was sitting in front of a rather ornate mirror. She was even more beautiful than he'd imagined. He was behind her in the mirror. She seemed to be enjoying his discomfort and slight awkwardness. She smiled and said, "Doctor, is there something wrong? Do I appear to be sick?"

John, blushing, answered, "No, madam, you look fine to me. I must admit that I just wanted to meet you. I have been to most of your performances, and after each performance, I have noticed an older gentleman with you."

"He enjoys my singing; he is my father," she said. Suddenly she stood and faced John. She looked into his eyes as if she were studying him. "Doctor, I noticed your English accent. I am French, but don't worry—I don't get involved with politics." She hardly had a trace of an accent, he thought.

John smiled. "I am glad. I promise never to discuss politics with you."

She returned his smile. "Are you that doctor who has been bringing exotic medicines to Boston from the Orient?"

"Yes, my father and I have conducted quite a bit of research into Oriental medicine."

She looked at him with great intensity.

"Are you a great doctor? I have been all over Europe, even to your England, and no one has been able to help me."

Startled, John asked in a concerned tone, "What seems to be the problem?"

"I have headaches; they come without warning. They seem to come with certain sounds and conditions. So far, they seem to be starting with the sharp sounds that come from a thunder-and-lightning storm. They are so painful that I have trouble standing. They last for hours sometimes. Do you think you can help me?" she said anxiously.

"I don't know yet, but between my father, who is also a doctor, and myself, I think we can find out what is causing these headaches and design a program to bring you relief, if not eliminate them. I think we are good diagnosticians, and we have progressed far beyond today's standard medical procedures. We do this by utilizing proven Oriental remedies to promote healing, as well as some standard methods. I will need to take a thorough history to help pinpoint the cause of your headaches. Can you come to our offices?"

"Yes, and I hope you can help me."

"Miss Morrell, I think we can."

"When should I arrive? I see by your card that you are somewhat outside of Boston."

"We will make time for you at your convenience. But the sooner, the better."

"How gracious of you. Are you coming to Saturday's performance? I will clear my schedule for possibly Monday or Tuesday. Come to my dressing room after Saturday's performance, and we will decide which day. Don't worry about Jacque; he is my guardian. My father insists on my protection. But I love Jacque as if he were my brother. He goes everywhere I go."

"That's fine." John was dazzled, but he was sure her interest in him was only professional—well, not totally.

"Sure, I'll be here on Saturday. Don't worry; we will figure it out."

"I am sure you will." Louise was smiling. "Au revoir."

John left. Jacque was just outside the door. He gave John a quick smile and turned away.

John attended the performance on Saturday. Louise was spectacular as usual, except near the end of her performance, an electrical storm developed. The thunder and lightning were exceptionally loud and sharp. The piercing sound of the thunder could be clearly heard in the theater. John carefully watched Louise during her last aria. She was very pale. He could see she was in pain. She finished beautifully but did not stay on the stage to enjoy the usual standing ovation. Jacque immediately rushed to her. She had collapsed behind the curtain. Jacque quickly picked her up and took her to the dressing room. John caught up with them in front of the dressing room. Jacque quickly opened the door. She screamed, "Jacque, get the laudanum." He got it quickly from the cabinet. John grabbed the towel. Jacque stayed right beside her, looking very worried.

"Louise, we've got to drown out that thunder."

She lay moaning on the couch. Her pulse was racing. She kept saying, "Mama, don't die."

"Jacque, we've got to wait out this storm," John said quietly. "I think I can do her some good back at our facility. We have plenty of room for both of you. I am going to the hospital to get some different medicine for her. It is close by, and my carriage is out front."

"Please hurry, monsieur."

John grabbed the opium out of the pharmacy. However, when he returned, the storm had passed. Louise was standing and smiling, as was Jacque. She laughed with relief that it was over.

"John, you are soaked."

"It is all right; I am just glad you are over this episode."

"Yes, John, I am over it."

"Louise, I want you to pack up, and I will meet you at your hotel on Monday morning. I think I have a good idea of what the cause is. I need a lot more information before we can go forward."

"John, I hope you are right. I was barely able to finish tonight, and if that dreadful storm had continued, I would still have that terrible headache." On Monday morning, promptly at ten o'clock, John brought the carriage up to the entrance of the Hotel Victoria. He couldn't believe what he saw: at least eight large trunks and a wagon to carry them. She had hired the wagon and two strong young men to load and unload them.

"John, the season has ended, and I would like to stay with you as long as it takes. Don't worry; I can pay."

"When you make your mind up, you mean it."

"Well, John, I had Jacque do some quick checking. Everyone he contacted, mostly at the hotel last night, confirmed that you and your father are the best diagnosticians within a thousand miles. That is good enough for me. I won't get in the way; I know you have many patients. Just see me when you can. Don't look so puzzled, John. I know you can do it."

"Louise, we will do our best. As I mentioned, I have some clues I want to check out." John's mind raced over the possible causes. He knew it was partly psychological. She blamed herself for her mother's death, but there was more—some weakness in neurotransmission. As John considered Louise's situation, he thought of an esteemed

Japanese colleague who'd helped in similar cases. *Dr. Segamoto will know the answers,* he hoped.

When Louise arrived, the sight of the clinic was overwhelming to her. The thirty-five-room mansion now included an addition that John had specially designed. The main feature was a beautiful room with tall, wide windows on all three sides. It gave John a spectacular view of the ocean to the east. The windows to the south and west provided great views of the tall, ancient oaks. Some were more than eighty feet tall. He loved the ocean sunrise.

Quietly, Louise entered the room. "You must be very proud of your home."

"Well, Dad and I share it. He lives in a portion of the north wing; I have part of the south wing. He is traveling the Orient right now. This gives him the opportunity to find new or time-tested procedures and possible medicines for our clinic. He should be back soon."

Louise, smiling, commented, "John, I see you don't depend on your practice to pay the bills."

"That's true, but we spend a lot of time with our patients. We do whatever it takes to get them well. They come from all over the country and, of course, locally. We do not advertise; we do, however, publish some of our cases and scientific findings in the top medical journals—at least the ones that accept us. This is what inspires some physicians to send their hard-to-diagnose-and-treat patients to us. Many times we do not charge any fees, or we charge very little. Remember, some of them spend all they have just to get here. Also, we have MD specialists on staff and eight other staff members, mostly staff nurses. We are a team with the same goal: successfully diagnosing, treating, and preventing disease, especially degenerative disease. We do a lot of work with herbs and many plant extracts. We are getting great data and medicines from South America, China, and Japan. The Japanese equivalents to our biochemists believe there is a relationship between a human body's electrical transmission process and the essential movement of vital chemicals that allow a person to function physiologically. Actually, we are trying to put many hypotheses together with credible, controlled, safe experiments to find ways to prevent the body from developing degenerative diseases, such as cancer, diabetes, heart disease, and many more. Louise, to put your mind at ease, we are getting close to discovering the causes of many kinds of neurological conditions, including headaches like yours."

Louise settled into a huge, well-furnished room with a great view of the sea. It had a balcony and a mounted telescope. Jacque had an equally appointed apartment. It was a beautiful Saturday morning. Louise let John know that she wanted to ride Jasper, the big black stallion, and paint the oaks.

"How did you know? One of my favorite ways to relax as well. I'd like to see your work sometime," John said.

"I did pack some of my paintings along with my oils," Louise commented. "How about you? Did you paint the oaks?"

"No, just the sea, but the oaks are my next project. The view from my window has inspired me. Louise, I will rig up a carriage when you are ready, and we will explore some places I haven't shown anyone," John exclaimed.

"John, I will look forward to that experience."

"Louise, have a grand day. I have arranged a picnic lunch for you and Jacque. See you tonight at supper at seven. Is that going to work for you? Hope you make it; Dad is due back tonight, and I want you to meet him."

"I'll be back." Louise smiled. "See you tonight; I am looking forward to meeting him." Louise and Jacque trotted toward the cliffs. It was unusually quiet except for the distant roar of the ocean. "What do you think of John, Jacque?" Louise asked.

"Well, he is certainly bright, and he seems to care about you."

"You mean as more than just an interesting challenge?"

Jacque laughed. "Oh, I think you know the man is beyond seeing you as just a patient."

"Yes, I can sense that. I mean, what sort of a man is he?"

"I think he is discerning and brave enough to withstand the anger he and his father are producing among the local physicians."

"Why anger? They should be happy to share in the knowledge John and his father bring to the art of healing."

"It doesn't work that way, Louise. Jealousy is a real and powerful reality. At this point, I don't think John and his dad realize the depth of the anger the medical community has toward them."

"If that is true, they are in real trouble. Yet somehow I know he will prevail. We must be over three hundred feet above the ocean up here. Look at those ships. They are so beautiful. Looks like two of them are racing toward the harbor. What do you think, Jacque?"

"You are right. I wonder if John's dad is on one of them. That one is one of their ships, and it is pulling ahead."

"How do you know it is one of John's ships?"

"Well, it is flying the Lunt flag. See the blue *L*?"

"Oh, yes, I wonder if it is coming in from Japan."

"I don't know. I hope it has the stuff you need for your headaches. Louise, let's take a look at the oaks. John seems to think they are nearly petrified."

Louise smiled. "I hope not. They are huge, beautiful, and very much alive."

"Look at those fallen branches and tree trunks. They look petrified to me. I hear the gales here are very severe," Jacque intimated. "These trees really catch it up here on the cliffs."

"Look, there is John's special addition. He has quite a view from that room. The home is high enough that the addition is on the first floor. It is surely at least sixty yards from here. That large window catches the sun and makes it sparkle. Look, there is a large oak towering over John's addition."

"Louise, we had better get back. This forest is quite large. Do you see a setting you would like to paint?"

"Yes I do. There is something mysterious about this forest. I need to find out what it is."

They arrived at the stable at three o'clock that afternoon. John was waiting for them in front of his special addition.

"I saw you two out there. I am glad you are back. You might have noticed the *Sea Cloud* pulling ahead of our rival, the *Sea Witch*. My telescope showed me that we were ahead of the *Sea Witch* by several lengths. Dad and Captain Jacobs, skipper of the *Sea Cloud*, will be here soon. You and Jacque are in for a treat if you like great sea stories. Oh, by the way, today is the captain's birthday. This is his thirtieth year on the high seas, and his tenth year with our company. He is always on time or faster. That is important in this business. We must stay ahead of the competition, you know."

"John, I am looking forward to this special celebration. How shall I dress?"

"Louise, you look beautiful in that white evening gown with all the ruffles."

"Oh, John, it's so old. But if you wish, I will wear it."

"Well, it is semiformal. I'll be in my dark blue waistcoat. You will be beautiful in any costume you choose. I hope you will feel quite at home; I have arranged for a fifteen-piece orchestra. You know them all. They are musicians from the music hall."

"You must be kidding. You mean that you want me to sing, don't you?"

"If you want, it would be wonderful if you would perform one or two of your songs. Do you mind?"

"I'd be happy to," Louise said, smiling. "But I am going to sing them to you. I hope I embarrass you."

"You won't. That will be an experience I will cherish. I hope they all think you mean it."

"I always sing to people who mean something to me."

"I do believe you are flirting with me, Louise."

"John, how could you tell?"

CHAPTER 2

The Lunt mansion's dining hall was impressive. At least two hundred guests flowed into the great dining room. Captain Jacobs seemed to know all the guests. The crowd included captains, first mates, seamen, merchants, doctors, lawyers—a whole cross section of Boston society. Some ministers were also in attendance. These ministers were respected and loved by nearly everyone in the shipping community. They were the ones who gave final tributes to sailors lost at sea due to storms or tragic mishaps. They had the task of comforting the sailors' wives, children, mothers, and dads. These pastors prayed for safe voyages and for the men manning the ships. The sailors remembered this kindness, and many of them gave thanks to their Lord and to the pastors who cared enough to pray for them. They and their families attended church regularly when they were not a sea.

There were three great tables in the dining hall, each reaching nearly sixty feet. The chairs were made of fine wood and cushioned with deep purple velvet. The tablecloths were made of the finest Irish linen. The aroma that filled the hall was of venison, rich brown gravy, several varieties of vegetables, lobster, and many kinds of fish. Each table was full of silver serving dishes. Goblets of cider and many kinds of breads added variety.

The Lunts, Captain Jacobs, Miss Morell, and four pastors sat together at one of the tables. Pastor Charles Sloan gave the blessing. He was a huge man with a mane like a lion and a full gray beard. He said, "Dear Lord, we thank you for what we are about to receive. We thank you, God, for your protection for the men who labor on your seas and the many blessings we all receive because of your love and mercy. May this be a joyous occasion for Captain Jacobs on his birthday, and may he serve this community many more years to come. Amen." All present repeated, "Amen."

They all ate their fill. The talk was of the sea. The merchants especially enjoyed stories from Captain Jacobs. Many old friendships were renewed, and new friendships were begun.

Louise was resplendent in a pure white gown. Her complexion, slightly dark, really shone. John was very proud to have her by his side. His father, Evan, commented, "John, she is exquisitely beautiful."

"I know, and she is going to sing for us. What do you think, Captain?"

"I think she is wonderful, and I too have heard her sing. Thank you both."

"Well, Louise, the orchestra is ready."

"John, I am honored." Louise left the table and whispered to the conductor.

John stood. "Ladies and Gentlemen, I give you the wonderful Louise Morell." A huge round of applause broke out. The audience stood. The orchestra started. She sang an aria from *La bohème*. The reaction at the end was joyous applause followed by loud appeals for an encore.

She turned and looked squarely at a very happy Captain Jacobs and said, "Captain, this song is dedicated to you and all the brave seamen and their families." She sang with great emotion "How Great Thou Art." At the end, men and women were crying. There was an awkward silence, and then the hall exploded in applause. Many rushed to Louise to thank her. John went to her, smiling. Captain Jacobs and the pastors were also smiling and were elated.

Pastor Sloan approached Louise and said, "That's what this town and nation need now. I have never heard that hymn sung so beautifully and with such emotion."

"Thank you, Pastor. It was a pleasure to see the outpouring of love."

"John, I don't think I've ever been so moved," Captain Jacobs said. "Louise, we all love you. Not just because of your voice, but because we can see that you care for us."

"That's right," chimed in Evan. "That kind of love and dedication is the most powerful medicine there is."

"I agree," said John. "We would like to have you help us here."

"What can I do? I'm just a singer. I do love the people here—so different from people in Europe. These people seem to appreciate everything. I feel a wonderful energy coming from them. It is like electricity. I want to sing to them. It is just a deep, warm experience for me. John," Louise whispered, "I am exhausted; I need to rest."

"Of course, tomorrow is Saturday. Let me walk you to your room." John and Louise walked slowly down the hall. "Louise, I want you to know that you are a great inspiration to me. I have never been happier. Just thinking about you makes me happy. I don't want to rush things, but I do hope we can get to know each other better."

"You make me happy too, but I am not sure I fit in here. You have it all—a meaningful profession, a whole town that cares about you and your father, and this wonderful place of healing. John, I'm very tired. I've got to get some rest. Good night. See you in the morning."

Louise slept in the next morning, and later, when she woke up, John joined her for breakfast. He was excited to see her, and at the end of breakfast, he said to her, "Louise, when you sing, it is like a healing prayer. My father and I have been studying the power of prayer to help very sick patients. They are truly anxious and many times depressed. We think there is a link between the stress of anxiety and depression and negative physiological changes in biochemistry. This kind of stress definitely inhibits the healing process. Louise, the pastors are sure this is true. That is why they are invited here. They pray with these patients and have their congregations pray for them. They pray for all of us here at the clinic. Louise, I can feel it. Sometimes, after a long day of seeing patients, I am so exhausted that I can't sleep. I usually go to the library, which is really a depository for our current research and the research we have accumulated from around the world over the years. Last night, after I left you, I was reading, and a problem that had been eluding me about Mr. Jeremiah Little, one of my patients, began to become clear. I was led to research I thought I had forgotten, and the rest of the puzzle unfolded. As I told Dad this morning, some sort of power led me to the answer. Dad said, 'I want you to know that last night every seat in our chapel—all 150 of them—was filled, and more people were in the overflow area.' Louise, they prayed all night for Mr. Little and me."

John and Louise left the table and began walking in the garden. John continued as they walked, "Early this morning, I hurried to Mr. Little's bed. His fever had broken, and his breathing had improved. I was amazed and immediately went to the chapel to announce to the pastors and the others there that Mr. Little was much improved. They seemed strangely at peace. I told them I wanted them to know that their prayers worked. I told them, 'Mr. Little is much better. His fever has broken, and with your prayers, a solution came to me late last night. I'm going to continue to use it. It was as if some power were guiding me through the tomes and scientific papers. I thank you for your prayers.'

"Louise, Allen Little, the brother of Jeremiah Little, stood up. He sobbed, 'You are a great healer, but God is the greatest healer. We are thankful to you for being an instrument of God for my brother.' I was very moved by what he said."

Mr. Little did recover. He had a severe case of dysentery. John thought at first it was typhoid fever. His research eliminated that diagnosis. Nevertheless, he did feel the power of those prayers and was truly thankful for them.

"I'm glad you told me about Mr. Little and the people who prayed for him. I would like to help here, but I'm confused somewhat. I'm an internationally known singer. Should I give that up now?"

"Let's pray about it. I've been a man of science only. I didn't think there was room for religion, but, Louise, this isn't religion. It is a relationship with God. I want and need that. I've had to see people die here, and many of them, in their last hours, prayed that I would become a Christian, that I would trust Christ as my savior. I did just that, and so did Dad. It's made a difference in my way of doing things and how I view life and people. I care not only about them as patients but about their relationships with God. Someday we all must die. This life is like the blink of an eye compared to eternity. What we do on earth for God is important."

"I want you to know I've seen a real caring attitude in you, your dad, and the staff. I knew it couldn't all be just extreme professionalism."

"They are people who are in the hands of God, and they know it and live it. It brings them peace and direction. I feel God has led you to me and this place."

"I feel that way too. I have for some time. I grew up in France. I never experienced the warmth and closeness that I feel here."

"Louise, would you like to trust Christ as your savior? I believe He is moving you in His direction."

"Yes, John, I believe you are right. Can you help me do this?"

"Yes, there is a prayer that goes something like this: 'Dear Lord Jesus, I know that I am a sinner. Thank you for dying on the cross for my sins. Please forgive me and save me.' If you mean this from your heart, God will forgive you. You will forever be His, and He will guide you, love you, and never forsake you. You will be saved."

Louise bowed her head and quietly asked the Lord to be her savior. She looked up at John and smiled.

"I am so glad for you," he whispered. They put their arms around each other. "I love you, Louise."

"I love you too, John," she answered. "I have never been happier. Please let me join you in this work. I know I can help."

"I'm so proud of you. I know you can too. I have something else that you will need. After I trusted Christ, I began reading the Bible. I started with the Gospel of John. Reading the Bible is one of the ways God talks to us. It's really great. Would you like to start too?"

"John, I don't have a Bible."

"That's not a problem; I have an extra one. Let's meet tomorrow morning in my study."

"Yes, John, I will look forward to it."

"We'll have breakfast at eight and go from there. I have a whole day off. We'll go for a ride after. Now I want you to rest before we get ready for dinner."

"I want to tell Jacque and everyone."

Just then, Jacque burst into the hall, startling both of them. "John, there is a Dr. Joshua Crill here to see you. He says it is very important."

"Thank you, Jacque. Please take Louise to her room. I will join you both soon."

John went to the north door and led Dr. Crill into the library. Louise and Jacque, somewhat confused, left through the west door, headed toward her room.

Dr. Crill, looking very upset, stammered, "Doctor, you've really put yourself into a disgraceful situation. It appears that you have a patient here, Miss Morell, that has a possible brain tumor, and you have refused to have her examined by our neurosurgeon, Dr. Samuel Cruthers. Rumor has it that she lives here with you. Most disgraceful. Her father has been in Boston for a week. He wants answers, and so does the Boston Medical Society. You have avoided us for too long—you and your father. Well, you're not going to get away with it this time."

"Well, Josiah, looks like you and your cronies are really getting bored. For your information, Miss Morell is our patient, and if I thought she had a brain tumor, what would be accomplished by sending her to you? Not that your man is not capable. But don't you think Dr. Schuler in New York, who is known as the best in the business and has written more books on the subject than anyone, would be her best chance?"

Dr. Crill looked stunned. "Your disloyalty is outrageous, Doctor. Her father is in town. He just arrived last week from France. He landed in Boston and was shocked to hear about Louise collapsing on stage. He knew about the headaches. Her father inquired about her at the hospital. He talked to Dr. Cruthers. He demanded that his daughter get the treatment she needs immediately at our hospital. We told him about this outpost for Far Eastern poppycock called advanced medicine."

"Dr. Crill, I would be glad to debate with you, but I think after I meet Mr. Morell, he will agree with me that the best course of treatment for his daughter will not be found in your hospital. I have treated patients who chose to come to us after your people misdiagnosed them and performed unsuccessful treatments, including surgeries. Dr. Crill, you just don't want our clinic to exist, and you are trying to use Miss Morell as a way to gain the power to disrupt us—or even eliminate us—because you see us as competition." John was outraged and moved toward Dr. Crill, glaring at him. "I think, Dr. Crill, that this interview is over."

Stammering, Crill said, "Dr. Lunt, you have made a grave mistake. You and this facility of yours are going to be destroyed." Sneering, he continued, "I am going to make sure you and your gang of incompetents are through."

Suddenly Jacque appeared. "I don't know who you are, sir, but you are wrong. I demand that you apologize to Dr. Lunt immediately."

"I will not. Who are you?"

"I am Jacque LaForet, the finest swordsman in all of France. I am protector of Miss Morell and her father. Sir, unless you withdraw your threat and apologize, consider yourself formerly challenged to a duel tomorrow morning at dawn."

"Jacque, that will not be necessary," Louise said as she entered the room. She was in tears. She had heard the last part of the conversation between John and Dr. Crill. Her posture became rigid, her face very pale. "Dr. Crill, I want you to know that I have every confidence in John and his father. It's easy to see that you are a small-minded, jealous man interested only in your own aggrandizement at the expense of anyone you fear is in your way."

"Miss Morell, how dare you talk to me in that tone."

"Don't you understand? You are not welcome here. I will never go near your hospital. John has never said anything derogatory about you or your hospital. You, sir, are not a gentleman. I do not appreciate you trying to poison my father against John and his father."

"You'll be sorry, young lady. You can't fight the power of the Boston Medical Society."

"That's quite enough, Doctor. You have openly threatened Miss Morell in front of witnesses. I would leave now before you are forced to meet Jacque on the field of honor."

"You haven't heard the last of this." Crill stormed out of the room in a rage, muttering to himself.

Louise, still shaken, turned to John and said, "Well, that was an experience I will not soon forget. What a despicable little man."

John smiled at her. "Yes, he is hard to like. I should have sensed those feelings at the hospital."

"John, I must see my father as soon as possible."

"Yes, and you will. I feel terrible about this. I will send my people to locate him and bring him back to you."

"I will go also," Jacque exclaimed.

"Only if you promise not to challenge the good doctor to a duel."

Jacque laughed. "John I think he would die of fright before I drew my sword."

"Take the rig, and put the two mares on it. They are fast. I know you can convince Mr. Morell to come back with you."

"I would head for the Boston Towers. That is where he stays when I am in concert," Louise said.

"I know," said Jacque. "We will be back by this evening or earlier."

"John, I am so sorry to bring this on you. I don't understand people who hate like that."

"Louise, I don't really either, but we've got to straighten your father out. Your father does not know me. Is he going to trust that we can cure your headaches? He has heard a lot of negative comments about my dad and me. Will he believe them?"

"No, I think all of what that dreadful doctor had to say is obviously not the truth. Dad is too smart for the likes of him. He just wants to see me get well and be sure I'm in good hands. I am confident that after you talk to him and we tell him about us, he'll be fine."

"Can I tell him I love you and want to marry you?"

"John, you proposed? I do love you, and the answer is yes."

John replied, "Now I am the happiest man alive."

"Let's tell him together. You realize that we've only known each other three weeks."

"Yes, dear, but I know this is love, and I want you to be my wife."

"Oh, yes, John, I am sure of this. I've felt this way for most of the time we've been together."

"Actually, the first time I saw you perform stirred me."

"Really, John?" Louise smiled. "Come here." She kissed him slowly, and John was intoxicated with her warmth and special perfume. Her flaming red hair flowed over her fair shoulders. She was beautiful in every way.

CHAPTER 3

It was seven o'clock in the evening, and John and Louise enjoyed a wonderful supper, just the two of them, out on the main balcony. They looked into the distance and saw a small speck moving quickly with a dust plume behind.

John and Louise readied themselves to meet Jacque and her father. The carriage arrived in ten minutes. Her dad was smiling. "Well, my darling daughter," he said in French, "you have some explaining to do."

Louise rushed to meet her father. "I know you don't believe that horrible Dr. Crill," she said as she threw her arms around him.

"No, but I'm not a medical man. They had me convinced for a while that you were being held against your will. You know, John, Crill is going to try to destroy this clinic. He especially dislikes Oriental medicine and the fundamental preachers you continually invite to this clinic. They say you are experimenting with the supernatural. What is that all about?"

"Well, sir, the pastors you are talking about are doing supernatural things like praying for and with our patients. We can see a difference; those patients are recovering faster than the others who are not interested in getting prayed for."

"Dad, there was a patient of John's who was very sick. John couldn't sleep and went to his library to try to find a cure for him. He has over a thousand books and scientific papers."

"It is true, sir; I didn't think Mr. Little would be with us by morning. It seemed that some force led me to several books and papers I had forgotten about."

"Dad, what John didn't know was that one of those pastors had brought over 150 people, including Mr. Little's family, to the clinic chapel to pray. At eight a.m., Mr. Little's fever broke. John was pleasantly shocked at seeing the great group of people that had been up all night praying for Mr. Little and John. Mr. Little fully recovered. John felt the power of all the prayers."

"When that gets back to Dr. Crill and the hospital, they will be enraged," Mr. Morell commented. "John, when I was in Boston last week, I did some checking. That hospital is very highly respected, and the feelings against you and your father are strong. They have the Boston Medical Society on their side, as well as the mayor of Boston. Somehow Miss Morell is the rallying cry that has them in a mob-like rage. They believe John is going to kill Louise with Oriental techniques."

"They think that we are not practicing medicine utilizing the modern science of today. Their minds are completely made up that my dad and I are terribly out of place and counter to everything they were taught about healing."

"I see Louise is still visibly shaken," her father muttered.

"John, what is going to happen? That terrible Dr. Crill and much of his hospital staff really want to hurt you and your dad," Louise said, beginning to sob.

"Louise, the real reason Crill and his cronies are in a rage is because they cannot stand the reality that they are losing patients to us. They have taken hospital privileges away from both of us. Neither of us can admit patients."

"Can he stop you, John? I mean, he sounds like he has a way, and he wants to use me as an excuse."

"Yes, he does. He and his cronies are going to declare that I am not capable of treating your condition, when I am quite sure they have no idea what is causing your headaches. Louise, do you trust me?"

"Yes, I do."

"There is a Japanese practitioner who has had great success with every kind of pain, including headaches. I want to take you to him. We can leave on the *Flying Cloud*. It leaves Boston the day after tomorrow for Japan." John was standing and looking deep into her eyes. "Louise, I love you. "Will you marry me right away?"

"I love you too, John." Without hesitating, she said, "Yes, I will. Do you mean tomorrow, John?"

"Yes, I can get all the particulars taken care of in the morning. We can be married by late afternoon tomorrow."

"Oh John, this is not how I dreamed it would be, but I understand the urgency. They can't get at us then, can they?" Louise prayed silently, *Lord, this is so sudden. I do love John. Please tell me this is right for both of us. Help me to trust John and know that you will protect us. I am so happy he loves me.*

"Dad, can you get this done for us? I mean, the license?" asked John.

"Yes, Son, but I'm going to use the old courthouse at the southern end of town. It's closer, and I know the people there."

"I've got a better idea: get the two of us to the courthouse to sign the marriage license, and if you can bring Captain Jacobs back to the mansion, he can serve as the legal chaplain and we can be married right here by him."

"You're right, Son. I'll make the arrangements with the captain. You and Louise get to the courthouse at four p.m. tomorrow. I'll write a document that will hopefully get the license prepared quickly."

The judge at first was startled at seeing John and Louise. John, smiling and without a word, handed him the documents his dad had written, and then the judge signed the marriage license. They arrived back at the clinic at seven o'clock that evening. John's dad and the captain were waiting in the chapel. John rushed to his room to get his grandmother's wedding ring, which she had left him for just this occasion. Louise was flushed but happy. John was somewhat nervous.

The captain was beaming. He had his Bible in his very large right hand. The ceremony was wonderful—short and to the point. The captain finally said, "I now pronounce you husband and wife. You may kiss the bride."

John and Louise held each other warmly.

Captain Jacobs looked seriously at John and Louise. "I suggest you leave that marriage license with your father. I suspect your enemies will try to prove you have kidnapped Louise."

"You're right, Captain." John turned to his dad. "All of our papers are in order, correct?"

"Yes, they are. Don't worry, Son. We can keep the wolves at bay. You get Louise well with your Japanese practitioner; we'll do the rest. Remember, Son, we have the best doctors and support staff in the Boston area. However, we are not going to make waves while you and Louise are gone."

Captain Jacobs quietly said, "I've got a surprise for you and Louise. I am going to captain the *Eagle* on your trip, and while you were busy, I ordered that the main stateroom be prepared for you two. She is the fastest and largest jewel in the fleet, built to withstand any weather. It is dark but only 8:30 p.m. I suggest that you and Louise secretly get on board tonight. She is sailing with the tide in the morning."

John's dad spoke. "John, Louise, we have taken the trouble to get the trunks packed for both of you. No less than four of our nurses rushed to pack Louise's trunks. I think you will find that the ladies have done a credible job."

"I trust them." Louise smiled. "John, let's get to the ship. I'll change into some traveling clothes."

"Great, Louise."

Captain Jacobs smiled broadly. So did John's dad as he said, "You two are going on a great adventure, and may God protect you."

"Thank you, Dad. Keep praying."

Jacque appeared at the door. "I am going also, yes? I am ready and packed. I only need my satchel."

"That makes sense. When they discover we have left, they will know Louise could not have been kidnapped, because Jacque would have stopped it."

John's dad added, "I also have a document signed by Jacque in front of witnesses, stating that he is accompanying Doctor and Mrs. Lunt and that she is with her husband willingly. John, I will only use this document if I have to."

The coach was ready, and two fast horses were hitched to it. It took a full hour to get to the docks. It was an exceptionally dark night. They arrived at 11:45 p.m., and there wasn't a soul near the ship. It was a four-masted ship, over 150 feet long. Everything went smoothly. Their departure was set for 6:00 a.m., or the first sign of dawn.

"John, this cabin is perfect. It's a grand stateroom."

"I'm glad you like it. Louise, it will take quite some time to get to Japan."

"John, this is so wonderful; come here." Their embrace was a great relief for them. At last they felt safe and protected. They left instructions not to be disturbed until the dawn departure. Captain Jacobs was pleased that all was progressing as planned and was happy for them both. He was satisfied not only because it was a joyous occasion for the two of them, but also because the cargo was one of the largest and most profitable yet.

They were shipping some very sophisticated equipment—machines designed for the production of large gears, some of which were on board. They were large and awkward to store in the hold. Also on board were the owner of the equipment, the inventor, and the main mechanic. The owner, Robert Holton, could speak and write in Japanese and Chinese. Mr. Holton, a mechanical engineer, was very involved in designing steam-driven oceangoing vessels. He had been to Germany, France, and England, conferring with top engineers who also felt it was time to utilize steam-engine technology in the ocean shipping industry.

CHAPTER 4

John and Louise seemed to glow. The *Eagle* was making wonderful time. The sky was a beautiful blue, and the wind was steady and fairly strong. The sound of the wind flowing through the lines sounded like music to John and Louise. Louise took to the ship quickly. She could hardly wait to learn about the ship. She enjoyed watching the crew add more canvas; it looked dangerous, especially when the ship began to heel over. One strong-looking sailor came down from the first mast very skillfully.

"How do you do that so quickly and effortlessly?"

"Oh, it takes effort all right, but fifteen years of experience helps."

"I see. Say, how fast can she go?"

"If the wind is right, up to eighteen knots. We don't add canvas in real heavy winds. Don't want to lose her masts."

"What keeps the ship from tipping over?"

"We have what is called ballast. There are heavy weights deep in the hold of the ship. It helps to have that heavy machinery down there also."

"When do you get to rest?"

"We work in shifts. Twelve hours on, twelve hours off."

"What do you do during your time off?

"We play cribbage, wash our clothes, and write letters to our wives or girlfriends. Many of us have written about you. We all heard you sing back in Boston. I hope you will sing for us again."

"I will as soon as the wind will let me, on some calm night."

Many had gone to her concerts. Many had also attended Captain Jacobs's birthday party and had heard her sing "How Great Thou Art." They loved her for being there for Captain Jacobs.

Captain Jacobs was the most respected captain in Boston, and they were the best-paid sailors on the East Coast. They also earned shares produced by the selling of the cargo or the fees paid to the company for safe delivery of the cargo. Captain Jacobs found Louise suitable clothing: seamen's trousers and a shirt. John also dressed like a seaman. Many times he involved himself in deckhand work. The men knew who he was and loved his help. Louise was invited to take the helm with John and the captain close by. She was in her glory with the wind blowing through her long red hair; her beauty was incredible.

One night, the wind died down, and all was quiet. "John, do you think the men would enjoy a few songs? I feel in the mood."

"Louise, I am sure they would be delighted. Where will you stand?"

"I can easily stand on top of the captain's cabin if you will help me up. They will be able to hear me from there, I think. I will give two performances so that all of them get a chance to hear." "That's wonderful. I'll make the arrangements. Captain Jacobs will be delighted." Word was passed, and the crew was elated. Captain Jacobs wasn't sure she would be able to project her voice.

However, the sea that evening was dead calm; there wasn't even a whisper of wind. John was excited not only because she was going to perform but also because Mr. Alberts, an engineer and an excellent violinist, had agreed to accompany her. Mr. Alberts had attended many of Louise's performances in Europe, Boston, and New York and was sure he could do a credible job accompanying her.

The sun was setting. The crew rigged up a candlelit lamp so that they could see her. She sang the songs she had performed in the opera house in downtown Boston. The men were so moved that some of them had tears in their eyes. She asked them if they had any favorite songs. One man wanted to hear her sing his favorite song, "An Irish Lullaby." She obliged. The engineer played a solo that was a classic at the end of the concert. He was excellent. There was no need for a second concert. The entire crew had attended the first one.

Later that evening, there was a slight change in the sea. The wind was picking up. Louise noticed that the moon was not as bright as usual, and there seemed to be a misty ring around it. "What does that mean, John?"

"Well, it usually means that we are in for some rain and possible rough weather."

"Captain Jacobs, what do you think?" Louise asked.

"Well, Louise, could be nothing, but we are nearing Cape Hatters, which is famous for treacherous waters, even in normal weather. Just to be safe, we are going to head out to sea to avoid that turbulence. We were averaging about thirteen knots before that short calm."

"I'm glad to hear that," John said. "Louise, there is nothing to worry about. Let's get some rest."

"Fine, I am tired. I must say that the engineer violinist was really good. He could be a soloist."

"Yes, he could, but he is more interested in ships powered by steam. It's not far off, Louise; I can feel it coming. Don't worry; I haven't heard of a steam-powered ship yet that could easily make it round the Horn. At least not like our four-master can. These steamers have a habit of seizing up or just losing power at the wrong time. It's true, however, that you can't stop progress."

The wind did pick up. As the ship headed out to sea, Louise seemed to enjoy the howling sound of the wind racing through the lines. She and John couldn't sleep. They watched the swells glistening as they broke in the night. "Louise, we are quartering the waves. It is very hard on the ship and crew. I think we had better get to our cabin."

"I am really hungry, John."

"Don't worry; the cook has prepared a special supper just for the two of us."

"How romantic," she said with a wink. There was lobster, venison, and a huge salad. "Oh John, this is wonderful." When they finished, Louise disappeared into the bath. She reappeared in John's bathrobe. Her beautiful hair flowed over her shoulders.

"It sure is great being out here. John, I hope you get a good rest on this trip. I know I am feeling very good." She smiled. "I think the men are very gentlemanly."

"They are the best, real professionals. All of them share in the profits of this company. Our system really works because they feel they are a vital part of this company. The safety of this ship comes first to them, and they know how to get every bit of speed out of her."

The next morning, the sea was higher, and the beautiful blue sky from the previous day had turned into a mixture of angry gray and black clouds. The ship careened forward. They reduced sail, with no apparent loss of speed. Louise was near the bow, enjoying the movement of the ship and the occasional spray and the crisp, salty air. John moved quietly and quickly to her side. He put his arms around her.

"John, it's fantastic."

"Yes, it is, but we are in for a big blow. Captain Jacobs is trying to stay ahead of it. I don't think he is going to do it. The crew is busy fastening everything down, and they are going to further take in more sail soon."

"Are we heading for anything unusual?"

"No, this is the best-prepared ship and crew on the eastern seaboard. I know everything will be fine, Louise. Let's get to our cabin, or if you wish, we can join Captain Jacobs and watch this storm develop."

"Please John, let's join the captain. I won't bother him."

Captain Jacobs was glad to see them. "Captain, how can I help?" Louise asked.

"Well, you can sing a sweet song to quiet this storm. I want to thank you for your performance last night. The men really appreciated it."

"You're welcome." Louise smiled.

"When this storm is over and we can hear each other, could you perform again? These men deserve a little bit of home."

"Captain, I would love it."

"That's great; I don't think you know how much you mean to them."

"Actually, Captain, I love them all."

"How do you make them feel you are singing directly to each one of them?"

"I am." Louise looked at John. "Except for that night our eyes first met. You were the one I was singing to then."

John flushed.

Captain Jacobs was very busy barking out orders to his first mate for a new tack. Louise said, "John, look at those waves; they are enormous. They seem to be cresting at least twenty feet."

"You're right; your engineer violinist is getting nervous. He wants me to go below with him to make sure all the equipment is secure."

"Do you have to go?"

"No, but he is a good customer. Don't worry; there is no problem."

"John, be careful."

John met Mr. Alberts below. He thought he heard something when the men were securing the hatches. John saw it first: one of the straps securing a giant gear had snapped. The gear was on a small but usually sturdy wheel, which made it easier to move the huge gear. John tried to put it out of his mind—the damage that two and a half tons of machinery could do. It could be considerable because it was situated near the stern. It was the biggest piece of machinery on board. If it broke loose, it could smash the hull.

John, the engineer, and the first mate decided to first put blocks on both sides of the wheels. The first mate brought four chains. The problem facing them was how to anchor the chains to the inside of the hull. John noticed that the motion of the ship was getting more radical. He went topside. The captain was concerned he could not outrun this gale, and it was getting worse. The barometer was dropping fast, which indicated more severe weather. The swells were over twenty-five feet.

"We're just going to have to ride it out; it's going to get worse," the captain said as he looked at John. Louise was trying to be positive, but she read the strain on the faces of John and the captain. John went below again. Louise wished he would stay with her. She heard men yelling, "The gear is loose!" One of the men from below came hurriedly to Captain Jacobs. He was terrified. "The gear has pinned Alphons! John is trying to free him."

At the same time, they heard a shout from below. "Alphons is no longer trapped. The radical motions of the ship freed him."

John saw that much of Alphons's upper body on his left side was crushed and bleeding. John managed to stop the bleeding; now he had to keep Alphons from going into shock. "Get blankets fast," he ordered. "We dare not move him yet."

Alphons was in great pain, and he was shaking badly and rapidly turning pale. Patrick, a friend of Alphons's, brought two heavy, rough grade blankets. John wrapped them tightly around Alphons, who stopped shaking within ten minutes.

The gear had turned the only remaining block into splinters. The gear seemed to be alive. It didn't seem to need the motion of the ship to move. The anchor bolts securing the straps had been pulled out of the oak interior of the hull.

The first mate came to John's side. "John, we're in a gale now, could be a hurricane. The captain has ordered all sails hauled in except the jibs. We're dealing with forty-foot waves and at least seventy-knot winds. Is Alphons going to make it?"

"I've stopped the bleeding, but he has many broken bones. Don't worry about Alphons; just keep that blasted equipment from sinking us! How fast can we drill some holes in those beams behind that gear?"

"I'll see, sir; I'll get the carpenters on it. They will risk getting crushed. But if they don't succeed in getting a line to secure the gear and keep it from moving, that monster could sink us. Look, we're shipping water."

As the men concentrated their efforts on patching the hull, they moved quickly and timed their work to avoid the deadly movements of the gear. The carpenters worked swiftly. It took thirty minutes to auger through the oak rib, one of the main structures of the hull. The gear, as if on cue, smashed into the hull. However, this time, the men took advantage of its position and firmly pressed it against the hull, near the beam. Now they had a chance to secure the gear. The task was like trying to subdue a huge wild animal. Eventually, the chain pulled the gear through the oak beam so that it could not move.

Alphons and John looked on with amazement. The repair work on the hull was accelerated without the danger of anyone being crushed. The sea stopped coming into the ship. The head carpenter, Stanley Miller, and one of his men built a sort of cot for

Alphons. They wrapped him in twine so that he could be kept level as they took him topside. The wind was howling, and the ship was pitching badly. The wind blowing through the multitude of lines made a terrifying noise. Even without the sails, the strain on the masts could be measured by their groaning. The lines were taught, and the seventy-knot wind made them sing like a symphony of desperately shrill music.

John and the seamen finally got Alphons to the deck and into the infirmary. Louise was there. She had been praying for the ship, John, and Alphons. Alphons had lost consciousness but was breathing regularly. He was no longer in shock. "Thank God!" John exclaimed.

Louise, tears in her eyes, held John close to her. She was scared, and she looked into his eyes for assurance. "Is that horrible thing going to hold?"

"Yes, and it takes more than two tons of iron to sink this ship. She's nearly all oak and built for the ice of the Antarctic."

"Oh John, I know we're going to be all right." She smiled.

They staggered to their cabin. John was exhausted, and so was Louise. Both fell into a deep sleep. Morning found them nearly one hundred miles off course. The wind was still strong, but much weaker than before. They stayed the course to Japan, traveling at full sail before the wind. The ship seemed to be in a race with the waves.

John got dressed and joined the captain. "We're making at least sixteen knots, John. The sea is in our favor. You know, you and the men below saved us. That gear could have stove in the hull, and we could have lost her. Is Alphons going to make it?"

"I think so. He's pretty broken up, but he's tough and was always very positive. I suspect most men would not have survived. Captain, you know we have to get Alphons to the closest port with a hospital."

"The closest port with a hospital is Fort Lauderdale. We will be there by morning."

"Good, he will make it with good medical attention, thanks to that engineer."

"How is Louise taking all this?" the captain asked.

"She is a wonder. She prayed for us a lot."

"You know how we all feel about her, John."

Sailing before the wind was exciting. The ship and the sea were as one. Louise was standing with John just outside their cabin. "I can't help getting the feeling Dr. Crill is up to something."

"Don't worry; Dad will be there. Besides, what can he do? We're not breaking any laws. The patients we take care of get the best care possible, and they would attest to that."

"I know. Are you sure your dad will be there to handle that man? I saw a dreadful evil in Crill's eyes, much like the commissioner of police in Paris."

"What happened in Paris, Louise?"

"He was attracted to me. He was a terrible man, married with three children. First it was flowers and then invitations to dinner. Finally, he was in my dressing room, waiting for me. He had a bottle of champagne on ice. He was drunk. I screamed for the police. He *was* the police. Fortunately, a stagehand burst into the room. He knocked the commissioner out with one blow to the chin. The stagehand was Jacque; he quickly dragged the commissioner out into the hall. When the commissioner awoke and saw Jacque, he was enraged. Apparently he did not know that it was Jacque who'd hit him. Nevertheless, he was furious. My father got word that he was going to punish my father and me. We had nowhere to turn; the commissioner could do no wrong and admitted to nothing. Fortunately, your dad, who attended most of my performances, found out about our situation and quickly made arrangements to get us on one of his ships bound for Boston. You didn't know about this, John?"

"Now I know why Dad insisted that I see this new French sensation. He was right. But I didn't know he was involved in your escape." John was smiling.

"Somehow I knew he was trying to get my nose out of the books to help me meet my future wife."

"Are you disappointed, John?" she said, smiling.

"No, I just wish I could have found you on my own."

"Your dad loves you very much, and he is a total romantic. That is why he is no match for the treachery that insanely jealous Dr. Crill is capable of."

"Louise, there is nothing I can do until we get back. If necessary, Dad will get a letter off to the Boston police."

"I hope he will," Louise murmured.

John, looking into her eyes, said, "You know I love you, and no matter what happens, we will make it. Please don't worry so. Whatever happens, it's in God's hands."

She smiled and said, "John, I'm new at this Christian life. I mean, I knew the basic idea as a little girl, but until you told me that it's a personal relationship between me and Christ, I had no peace about anything. I must talk to you more and read that Bible you gave me."

"God does not ask us to stay in the face of danger, but He does ask us to pray for guidance. He may have a way for us to face a situation that we could not imagine."

"Help me to be more trusting. It's just that I've seen so much hatred and pain in the world. It's hard for me to trust people. Yet you, your father, and your friends have changed all that."

"Do you think that everything that has happened to you, to us, is just chance?"

"No, you are right," Louise replied. "It's all God's work, isn't it?"

"Louise, remember that Satan will do all he can to destroy anything that is good and furthers the cause of Christ. But we have God on our side. Satan can win battles but not the victory!"

CHAPTER 5

Fort Lauderdale was small and primitive, but it had a substantial fishing village. There was no large docking facility, but John, Alphons, and Louise made the port in a small sailboat from the ship. There was a physician, Dr. Morgan, who ran a small clinic. He was capable and was used to patching up injured fishermen. He agreed with John that there were no internal injuries. John assured Alphons that he would pick him up on the way back, or he could purchase passage back. John gave him more than adequate funds to do what he saw fit.

Dr. Morgan was happy to get the money to take care of Alphons for a year if necessary. John and Dr. Morgan discussed medicine for over an hour. Both men agreed on many subjects. Dr. Morgan had graduated from

Harvard Medical School ten years ago. He had become a professor; however, because of his health, he'd decided to retire and write. As it turned out, his retirement didn't last. He was really needed and was loved by the local fishermen and their families. He had never married, and he seemed fit for a man his age.

John said he would help him with his clinic. They talked about Louise. They both agreed John was right; the Japan trip was the right decision. Dr. Morgan took to Louise like a father. He told her to keep trusting in the Lord. He assured her that Alphons would get well. He said he would pray for both of them. Alphons was smiling when John and Louise left on the little ketch. He knew he was in good hands.

"John, you knew that doctor, didn't you?"

"Yes, and I'm glad for it. He was my professor of anatomy at Harvard—a brilliant man. He left Harvard two years after I graduated from medical school. Soon after, I went back to London and joined my father's practice. Dr. Morgan suffers from arthritis and decided to retire, write, and move to a warmer climate. As you can see, he didn't retire. Lucky for Alphons that he didn't retire. Louise, I learned something important. Dr. Crill and Dr. Morgan were classmates at Harvard Medical School ten years before I arrived. Dr. Morgan said Dr. Crill was a fair student but was not well liked and had a nasty disposition, and Dr. Morgan believed he was mentally unstable. More than once he displayed a terrible temper. I'm beginning to think you are correct; Dr. Crill is probably up to something."

"I know; I can feel it. Maybe we should get back."

"No, Louise, I'm going to get you well with God's help. It's just a shame Crill is so angry. I know that progress does not come easily. It certainly did not in England. Someday there will be a way to bring together the best minds in all disciplines—including natural and traditional medicine, and biochemistry and biophysics—without the terrible hindrances of pride, greed, and politics."

"John, I hope so."

"I have thought about this concept. Someday total emphasis on the welfare of the patient will prevail, with medical practitioners utilizing the best of all disciplines. Just think of it, Louise—symposiums held in key locations around the world, teaching new methods and ways to convert theories into sound prevention and treatment systems. The new knowledge would have to be published in a way that it is acceptable to everyone. Do I sound idealistic?"

"No, it just sounds like a dream that you must pursue, and I believe that if anyone can make it happen, you can."

"You see, Louise, if there is an interdependence of bodies of knowledge pertaining to medicine, all positive approaches between nations will be used. Possibly, nations will also learn to get along because every nation will have interdependent goals and will need the contribution of others. I am convinced that ignorance is a catalyst for fear, hatred, and even war. Just think how wonderful it would be if there was a way to let nations know the importance of being able to bring the best minds together from all nations to harness the accumulated knowledge to solve real problems. That concept may be instrumental in avoiding misunderstandings and possible conflicts. It should not be who has the most power and knowledge but how it is shared and put into good use worldwide. The key is to be of one mind so that mutual trust exists and continues to build. That way, cultures, even though they are different in many ways, can share their strengths and work together to solve problems."

"I know you are right, John. I pray it will happen."

They were on shore only two and a half hours. John, Dr. Morgan, and Louise attended Alphons. The captain had more lumber for repairs brought on board, along with much fruit and other needed provisions. They made all the machinery below, including the rogue two-and-a-half-ton gear, very secure over the next few days.

They finally set sail. The men were in good spirits, as were Louise and John. It took forty-five days to reach the tip of Africa, Cape Horn. It was treacherous but very predictable. Captain Jacobs did not intend to get detoured by the fierce winds and difficult currents. To the captain's surprise, the raging wind subsided into a five-knot wind. It was nearly calm; the captain and John decided to celebrate rounding the tip of Africa. The night was full of stars, and the moon was especially bright. The food was exotic and plentiful. Captain Jacobs wanted the crew to enjoy the occasion. He asked John to invite Louise to sing for the men. She gracefully accepted. The sea was nearly still, and the moon illuminated the ship. John Haddon agreed to accompany Louise on his violin.

As she stood on the captain's cabin, dressed in her white evening gown, the men suddenly became hushed. Her gown seemed to glow. Many of the men were from Ireland. She started with "An Irish Lullaby." They all truly loved her. John could see this and was thankful and could see that Louise was energized by their attention. There was a strange bond between the men and Louise. She truly was their angel. For an ending, she started low and gradually reached the highest notes of the hymn "How Great Thou Art." Her head was leaning toward the heavens. Everyone was moved.

Captain Jacobs said a prayer, thanking God for looking out for them and asking for His mercy for the rest of the voyage. After a hardy amen from the crew, everyone who didn't have duties to perform turned in. The wind seemed to pick up at that moment.

Louise and John made their way to their cabin. Captain Jacobs caught up with them. Smiling, he said, "Louise, I want to thank you; that was a wonderful performance. Most of these men are married, and I'm sure they miss their wives, and the others miss their sweethearts. You bring them closer to God and, in that way, inspire them. I know because that is how I feel. Thank you."

Louise blushed. "That's the greatest compliment I've ever been given. Somehow a great peace came over me while I was singing. I know I wasn't alone up there."

John was just staring at her. He looked over at the captain. "We are blessed. These are times we will not forget."

"You're right, John. Say, that wind is picking up—got to get back to work. Good night, you two."

"Louise, you look tired."

"Yes, John, but I feel wonderful. John, this isn't going to end. I mean, I hope this great adventure continues. We can do a lot of good, you and me." She smiled broadly. "Please open our door and help me get out of this gown. It's not comfortable, believe me."

John exclaimed, "I'm not good at this, but I know I'll manage."

Louise smiled. They lay there in each other's arms. Soon they both slipped into a deep sleep. The morning was bright. They were sailing before the wind and gaining speed. The captain said they were now ahead of schedule and would be in Tokyo in fifteen to twenty days. The rest of the voyage went well. Louise enjoyed the porpoises swimming alongside the ship. John spent a lot of time with Captain Jacobs and the navigator as they tried to find ways to save time and distance. John wanted to stay a week in Hong Kong, the destination for much of the cargo. He worried that he didn't have time to get word to Dr. Segamoto that he was coming with a special patient, his wife.

The hurricane season was due to start in three months in parts of the Pacific. One of the important missions of the voyage was to pick up valuable cargo in Japan. They would first arrive in Hong Kong and then continue on to Tokyo, Japan. All the crew members were anxious to make port in Tokyo. They were welcome there, and they loved to buy exotic trinkets and beautiful clothing and fabrics for their wives, children, or sweethearts at home.

CHAPTER 6

It took ten more days to sail to Tokyo. John was anxious to get settled. Louise was dressed in a white summer dress. It was hot, about ninety degrees, and very humid. They rode to their destination on a rickshaw pulled by a little man who looked too old for the task. John spoke to him in perfect Japanese. The man smiled at Louise, and she smiled back. Louise could not believe the number of people as they made their way into the city. The odors of raw sewage and fish were prevalent. She smiled grimly. John was engrossed with pointing out various sites and landmarks to her.

As they progressed, the scenery became more rural and less populated, and there were fewer dwellings. There were several intricate, well-kept parks with little streams flowing through them. These parks were on multiple levels. They finally arrived at a fairly large, well-designed Japanese home.

"Where are we, John?" The mansion was four stories. John was smiling; he knew Louise was surprised. Two rickshaws carrying their belongings soon followed. They were guests of the British consul to Japan. Sir Alexander Duncan and his wife, Lady Julia Duncan, presided. Sir Duncan was a tall, mustached man of forty, angular and thin. He was warm and at ease with his position. "Louise, meet Sir Alexander and his very lovely wife, Julia."

"How do you do? I'm so glad to meet you." Julia smiled. "You must be tired; Jason will show you to your rooms. He will draw a nice hot bath for both of you."

"Thank you; you are right. We are a bit tired," Louise replied.

Julia was very beautiful and also tall but much younger than her husband. She was totally in charge of the household. She winked at Louise and said, "I want you to know you and John are our special guests."

John and Alex went off to make arrangements with Dr. Segamoto while Julia continued to talk with Louise. "They may talk Dr. Segamoto into coming here for dinner, but I doubt it," Julia continued. "He has literally hundreds of remedies—compounds of exotic herbs, rare plants, spices, and special water. And many technologies to make you well. Louise, you will be in good hands—just relax. I've been there just to make sure something isn't creeping up on my good health. He recommended that I get more rest. We entertain constantly, and some guests are not as pleasant as you and John. John is like family, so stay as long as you like. It's wonderful that John has found someone like you to get him out of his books and papers. He is brilliant, you know. I'm learning he also has compassion for people. They love him and his dad. Louise, I want you to know that John and his dad—because they are dedicated scientists and have used their wealth to scour the earth for remedies and have found cures—have enemies. Their enemies are men of lesser intelligence, but they are in powerful positions. Unfortunately, these are physicians and others with connections in government."

"I know what you mean. The chief administrator at Boston General, Dr. Crill, accused John of kidnapping me before they could operate on me for these headaches of mine. I'm so thankful I met John and his dad. Julia, John and I, as you know, left Boston in a hurry. Let me tell you the circumstance. My dad had just arrived in Boston from France. He was worried about me and immediately was directed to the hospital. I spent three hours in that horrid hospital in Boston. They told me

I probably had a brain tumor and that they wanted to operate as soon as possible. I didn't tell John that I had already visited the hospital. I had just met him."

"Louise, that doctor you named was a notorious scoundrel in London. He is a terrible man. He destroyed the reputations of several good doctors because he thought they were opposing him." "Does John know all this?" Louise uttered.

"I don't think so; Crill left London for Boston four years ago. My husband and John are friends. But I'm not sure they have communicated much lately. Alex told me about it, but he didn't think Crill would be in John's way for some reason."

"I've got to tell John about this," Louise stammered. "Of course, there isn't much we can do now."

"Well, you will be on your way in fifteen days or less."

"Yes, our ship must get back to Shanghai first to pick up the owner and the engineer of that dreadful cargo. I'm sure at least the owner is due back in the States. The captain will go to China to pick them up and load more cargo."

"I know he will not leave until he is sure you are healing. Don't worry about Crill too much. He can't really hurt you."

"I hope not. Isn't it terrible how men want to stop progress just to protect what they consider sacred? Julia, we will be leaving in two weeks or less. We have got to miss the hurricane season."

"You are right. I am sure your ship is being loaded now."

John and Alex came into the drawing room; both were smiling. John spoke first. "Louise, it is all set. Dr. Segamoto will see us tomorrow at five in the morning. He is only a half hour from here."

"That's great, John," Julia said. She then announced, "It is now five. How about supper at eight? Your wife and I have had a good talk. So don't spoil it with all your doctor talk."

"You're right, Julia. I just want a hot bath and some rest."

When she and John were alone, Louise said, "John, is it worse than we thought?"

"Louise, it doesn't matter as long as Dad is there and the clinic is intact. We will be just fine. Right now we are going to concentrate on getting you well."

Louise seemed to relax.

Supper was informal, and the food was wonderful. There were many Japanese delicacies and British corn beef and cabbage.

"Well, Alex, you and Julia, as usual, have really put on a great feast."

"You look a bit peaked, John," Julia observed.

"You are right. I am tired. Say, can we borrow a rig for tomorrow—about four thirty in the morning? As you know, Dr. Segamoto wants to see us at five o'clock."

"Of course, we're all anxious to see your beautiful bride get well."

Louise blushed and smiled at John.

"It is now ten. Let's all get some rest," Julia announced.

As promised, the carriage was ready. The horse was spirited and seemed anxious to get under way. Louise was nervous. "John, you know I trust you, but is there going to be pain involved?" She was frowning and looked frightened. He stopped the carriage.

"John, I'm curious. Have you dealt with Dr. Segamoto many times?"

"Yes, and he was able to work wonders with infectious diseases like pneumonia, ulcers, and many others. He is especially adept at pain. His knowledge of the nervous system is incredible. He is way ahead of us.

"Louise, I love you more than my life." He held her closely. "I will not let anyone hurt you."

As they approached what appeared to be a terraced garden with small, intricate waterfalls and many beautiful flowers, they were surprised to see exotic trees in full bloom. Suddenly the clinic appeared. It was much smaller than Louise had anticipated, but she was impressed by the Oriental beauty of it. The three-level clinic had a high swept roof covered with light red tiles. John and Louise were met outside the door by two lovely young Oriental ladies dressed in full costume. The taller one said in perfect English, "Doctor will see you now."

Dr. Segamoto, a small man with bright, dancing eyes, met them inside. He was in his sixties and seemed very spry. "Dr. John, you are welcome to accompany your wife."

"Thank you, Doctor." Louise was ushered into a small dressing room and was instructed to undress and put on a simple cloth gown. *This is really embarrassing,* she thought. *I wonder if John knows about this. Dr. Segamoto seems very professional.* She mustered her courage and said to herself, "I can do this." She quickly undressed and put on the gown. Meanwhile, John was talking to Dr. Segamoto.

Louise timidly returned and entered the room. The walls were lined with hundreds of bottles, all corked and filled with powders and liquids. John gently took her arm. "Dr. Segamoto, I want you to meet my wife, Louise."

"I am very glad to meet you. You are more beautiful than your husband was able to tell me."

Louise blushed. "Thank you, Doctor."

"So you are a singer. I also admire good music. We use it sometimes as part of therapy. Please tell me about yourself as far back as you can remember. John, it would be better if you were not present during this part of the examination. I will call you in soon." As if on signal, the two ladies appeared and led John out of the room. John smiled warmly at Louise to reassure her.

"Now, Louise, let's get to know each other. I want you to know that true healing must involve the mind, spirit, body, and nutrition. We also work with the electrical currents of the body. We must work together to bring all these factors into harmony. Certain conditions and pressures act to bring about disharmony. This can be brought about by toxic chemicals, traumatic incidences, constant mental stress, memories, and even certain noises. You and John have come a long distance, and I promise you I will do my best to put an end to your headaches. John has told me about your headaches, but I want you to tell me about them. When do they occur, for instance? In what part of your head do you feel pain? What is happening just prior to the pain? Does it stay in one place or move?"

Dr. Segamoto asked many more questions about the location of her pain. He was also interested in the levels and kinds of stress she may have experienced one hour before, and minutes before, the onset of the last headache. He asked her to describe the pain—for example, whether it was dull or sharp. He asked her to remember as far back as possible. "Have there been any traumatic or other incidents you have experienced?"

"Doctor, I watched my mother die of typhoid fever. It was terrible. I saw my father crying as she took her last breath. In her delirium, Mother said to me in her last moments, 'Sing for the world, and pray to God and He will use you.' I didn't understand what she meant until I met John. My mother died during one of the loudest and most terrifying storms I have ever experienced. It was seconds after a very loud crack of thunder and a bright streak of lightning that she gasped and died. Both my dad and I held each other and cried. Finally, the nuns came for her, and we were politely asked to leave. I remember that the lightning struck very near the little room we were in. I knew because the little olive tree outside was twisted and burned."

As the doctor listened, he turned and asked, "Was the window open?"

Louise answered thoughtfully, "Yes, I think so—just a crack for fresh air."

Dr. Segamoto was taking notes in a journal in English.

"After Mother died, I was in sort of a melancholy state for over a year. I didn't want to talk to anyone, even the priest. Then, one day, Father introduced me to Mrs. Trudo, a friend of his. She was a singer from the opera in Paris. She was very lovely and gave me a big hug. It felt so wonderful, as if my mother were there. Father started playing the piano in the parlor. Mrs. Trudo started to sing. It was beautiful, and I knew the song. She motioned for me to join her by the piano. We finished the aria together. My father was crying, and tears were in my eyes. I knew I could sing. Mrs. Trudo helped me.

"'You must come with me to the opera house tomorrow. Please, you have a great future,' she said.

"I was fifteen at the time, and I knew then that God had given me the talent to sing, but I needed training. Thanks to Mrs. Trudo, I got the best. The opera was very demanding. The stress was terrible. I lasted two seasons. My headaches became more frequent. They started to come during performances, just before my part. I would crave food, especially sweets, after a performance."

"What kind of food did you eat for breakfast, lunch, and supper?"

"I usually had toast and marmalade for breakfast. If I ate lunch, it was a light sandwich, broiled chicken, and coffee to drink. Supper was usually late, about eight or nine. It was a large salad with Italian dressing and a pastry for dessert. Father and I would walk until about ten o'clock and then retire. I do enjoy black coffee. I usually have two or three cups a day."

"How do you feel after the coffee?"

"I have more energy, and I feel more alert."

"Do you get your headaches during or after your coffee?"

"Come to think about it, I have them sometimes after supper."

"I see. How often per week does this occur?"

"At least once a week after I have coffee. Doctor, do you think there is a connection?"

"I am not sure yet. Do you drink alcohol, even wine?"

"No, I do not."

"Do you eat fish, crustaceans, beef, or pork?"

"Yes. On Sundays, after Mass, we would go to one of Dad's favorite restaurants and share a rack of lamb and specially prepared pork, vegetables, and a salad."

"Besides your headaches, do you ever feel tired after you have slept well?"

"Yes, sometimes."

"Does your stomach or abdomen ever ache between meals?"

"Yes, but it is just nervousness. I get nervous when I have to memorize my music. I get these headaches sometimes just before my rehearsals. Are you wondering about my involvement in killing my mother? I gave her that glass of water out of that well. She was fine until the next day. Then her health started to fail. I got that water out of the well. It was full of the fever. I did it."

Louise started to cry. She put her right hand to her head. "I'm sorry; it's back," she said. Louise fell to the floor. Dr. Segamoto called John to the room. Both doctors assisted her and put her to bed on the patio. She slept for three hours. Finally, John and the doctor entered the patio. Both men smiled.

John spoke first. "Louise, Dr. Segamoto is going to show us how to prevent your headaches. But there are several things that you must learn to do. It is not going to be difficult for you. You need to change your diet somewhat, and you will be on some natural compounds. Doctor is going to work on some pressure points."

"Louise, you have had a great shock, and you are not over it yet. We in the East believe there are electrical forces in our bodies that must be in balance for the human body to be in a state of wellness. I am going to demonstrate some techniques we use for diagnosis, prevention, and treatment. We are going to do everything possible to bring you into balance. Do not worry; I am also a graduate of Harvard Medical School and Japan's esteemed School of Neuroscience. I have also studied herbal medicine under the most learned masters. Your husband will be here with you. He will be treating you when you return home."

Louise was moved to the exam table. John had changed into a white coat. He had spent the last five minutes writing. Dr. Segamoto began palpating the area just below the sternum. John watched curiously. He asked John to place his hands in the same place. "Feel that?"

"Yes, I do," John replied. They continued the examination. They were activating several pressure points, trying to stimulate her electrical balance. The doctor spoke in Japanese. John read and spoke Japanese, so he was able to understand. Louise did not, so they could speak freely. The nurses translated their conversations into written English.

"Louise, now we are going to work on some other pressure points. It won't hurt. I'll be there with you so that I can learn."

Dr. Segamoto intervened again. "Louise, you are suffering from a traumatic incident that has interfered with your production of a chemical that controls pain. Also, the vascular system in your head is affected. This system becomes dilated and presses on the surrounding nerves. This causes pain. There are several conditions that precipitate these vascular headaches. They can be brought on by a loud noise, such as thunder or the sharp crack of lightning. John has all the techniques and compounds you will need. However, it is going to take time. Try to stay out of stressful situations. Let John handle it all. I would think that in a year or so you will be devoid of headaches."

"But, Doctor, that horrible Dr. Crill is waiting for us to return. I know in my heart that he is."

"Louise, don't worry about him; Dad is there. You are my wife. I'm not going to let anything happen to you. The doctor and I have some work to do. I won't be long. It's a beautiful day, perfect for a walk in the park just a small distance from here."

"You're right; the blossoms are beautiful, and there is a little brook I have heard about from the doctor. He recommended that I take a walk by it. He says he does quite often after a strenuous day. This has been a strenuous day. It is so beautiful here that I could stay for months. I am not looking forward to going home yet."

"I understand. I have learned a lot from Dr. Segamoto. It is going to take some time and much therapy, but you can look forward to a life without headaches. Just stay happy."

"I am, John. Thank you for bringing me here."

John ducked back into the clinic. Louise put on her new white dress and held a white parasol. She looked beautiful as she made her way to the park. There were exotic trees filled with white and pink blossoms.

Children were playing near the brook. There was an ornate little bridge over the brook.

John had been watching her for ten minutes. She was not aware of him back on the patio. She decided to cross the bridge with her parasol over her shoulder. It was a stunning sight; the sun's early evening rays shone on her flowing dress. She was smiling at the little children playing near the bridge. It was a picture he knew he would never forget. He loved the graceful way she moved and smiled at the children.

Soon John joined Louise in the park. He really enjoyed the total atmosphere, the smells, and the little babbling brook. They both seemed to unwind and relax. She was looking forward to the exquisite supper being prepared for them. The ordeal had brought back her appetite.

During the meal, Dr. Segamoto described the variety of fruits and vegetables, as well as the medicinal herbs and spices being served. There was a variety of fowl cooked in special spices, and, of course, hot tea was served. Soothing music added to the relaxed tone of the evening. The talk was of Japan's people, happy and content with their lives.

Following supper, Louise and John were led into separate rooms and asked to disrobe and lie facedown on well-padded tables. Louise had two ladies to assist her, and John had two muscular middle-aged men. The massages were wonderful. They later were told that they had experienced deep-tissue massages. They were told to drink much water, which was an important part of the detoxification process. Dr. Segamoto pointed out that there would be a change in the color of their urine for a short period of time as a result of the detoxification process and told them not to be alarmed. However, he said deep-tissue massage was important for good health and would be especially helpful for Louise's healing.

That evening, Jacque appeared. "Where have you been?" Louise asked, somewhat distraught but relieved to see him.

"I've mostly been with the crew. I like being with them. Besides, I really don't think you need my services any longer. You are married now, and John can protect you. I'm just in the way."

Louise responded, "No, you are not. We don't know what we are facing back home in Boston. Both of us fear Crill has been up to something."

"I think you may be right," Jacque exclaimed. "John, I came to tell you I have a wagon to carry the medicines you are taking back for Louise. Also, did you know that we are taking a large shipment of spices and medicinal compounds on this voyage? I think many of them will be useful for your clinic."

"That's very interesting. I've been looking forward to this. I would like to see that manifest."

"The captain thought you would; here it is."

"Thank you, Jacque."

"John, did you know we are scheduled to leave the day after tomorrow on the morning tide? If you wish, I'll help pack whatever you want and get it on board. When should I return for you and Louise?"

"Tomorrow evening would be fine, about seven. Thank you, Jacque."

Jacque looked happy as he left. Louise was glad he was going to stay with them at home. John was delighted with all the medicinal herbs, spices, and compounds on the manifest. He could stock several clinics with them, he thought. John knew Dr. Segamoto had made the selections as arranged. He decided that they were not all for his clinic. Many were to be shipped to Los Angeles. It was now a bustling city with many Asians and Westerners who were much more open to new ideas. John put that thought in the back of his mind.

CHAPTER 7

The voyage home was uneventful. Louise sang for the crew, and she looked and felt great. She and John spent a lot of time talking about how they would work together to improve and expand the outreach of the clinic. John thought it would be great to train physicians on the use of Japanese techniques and the use of other Asian medicines. They even thought about eventually starting up several more clinics all around the country. Louise thought about how she could help.

They got to Boston in record time. They were glad to get back. Mr. Morell saw them coming and met them with a carriage. He was obviously upset. "Crill," he exclaimed, "just got an injunction to close the clinic. The mayor, Crill, and the state district attorney joined forces. This action was based on their belief that you and your dad are guilty of practicing medicine outside the dictates of the Massachusetts Medical Society."

"Mr. Morell, please drive us to the clinic." John was very angry.

When they arrived, Crill and the sheriff had just finished nailing a two-by-four across the front entrance of the clinic. "Wait a minute, Crill. We live here. You can't keep me, my wife, and my dad from our private home," John shouted.

Crill snarled, "You and your dad are out of business. We'll see if you can live here."

"You horrible little man," Louise shouted. "Have you no shame? Where are John's equipment and medicines?"

Crill, glaring with a sinister smile, said, "You mean that illegal stuff now under lock and key?"

"You worm," John shouted. "That equipment and those medicines are nearly impossible to replace."

Crill retorted, "You should have thought of that earlier. I will teach you to try to change today's medicine with your mumbo jumbo. I hope you get the point—you and yours are not wanted."

"I have over four hundred patients who will disagree with you, Crill."

"Do you? We have taken the trouble to examine your records and have contacted each of them. I think we have convinced them that you are practicing medicine that is not legal, and if they want to sue you for malpractice, we would stand behind them."

"You haven't missed a trick, have you, Crill?"

"No, I haven't," Crill sneered. "You may get back in that house, but it will take weeks; I've seen to that. Don't try to cross me, John. I am watching you."

"I am going to do everything in my power to stop you," John shouted.

"John, what are we going to do?"

"Don't worry, Louise; I know how to handle him."

John was right. The next day, a federal marshal reopened John's home. The operation of the clinic was a separate battle. The marshal said he knew what they were up against. He told John, Louise, Mr. Morell, and Jacque that they were not safe with a man like Crill around. He advised them to move into town until John's New York lawyers could reopen the clinic. Louise and her dad stayed at Mr. Morell's hotel, as did Jacque.

Louise and her dad were lunching in the hotel dining room when Dr. Crill approached their table. "What do you want?" Louise exclaimed.

"Just to let you know it will do no good for your husband to bring in attorneys from New York City."

Just then, Jacque arrived. He stood over the little man. "Are you trying to bother Miss Morell and her father again? Crill, if you continue to harass these people, you will be in a duel with me some dark night."

"Are you threatening me, sir?"

"No, I am only inviting you to duel with me. That is not a threat; ask any attorney. However, if I happen to kill you during the duel, that would be too bad."

Louise was turning pale. The sight of Dr. Crill made her sick to her stomach. She collapsed. Almost as if on cue, four very large orderlies from the hospital pushed Jacque and Mr. Morell aside and put Louise on a stretcher. She was in the hospital within five minutes. Mr. Morell and Jacque were physically blocked from entering the hospital.

Crill, snarling, said, "Now we've got you, and your husband can do nothing about it. We are going to relieve that pressure on your brain. Don't worry; it is just a little drill we use," he said to himself.

Jacque screamed in the lobby, "If you hurt her, Crill, I will find you and kill you."

Louise awoke and seemed fine—no sign of a stomachache or a headache. Crill was standing near her bed. "Crill, I'm stating in front of this room full of doctors and personnel that I will not permit you to operate or touch me in any way."

Many of the men in the room were fans of Louise and looked at Crill as if he were an evil villain.

One young man spoke up. “Miss Morell, we won’t let that happen. We truly love you.” All fifteen men in the room agreed to protect her.

Crill was in a rage. “I’ll get her out of here,” he muttered in a low whisper.

That evening, Louise was gagged, sedated, and bound hand and foot and secretly put into an ambulance. Louise awoke in the horse-drawn ambulance. She was not alone. A very strong and determined nurse was attending her. Louise was strapped to a stretcher. Crill had declared her insane and was shipping her to an asylum not too far from John’s clinic. He wanted to make John suffer as much as possible. John’s lawyers could do nothing. Dr. Crill had judged her insane, and the decision stuck.

“I’ll take that gag out, but you must behave,” the ambulance attendant told her.

“Where are you taking me? I am so drowsy.”

“You’ll find out soon enough.”

They arrived at the asylum. It was a large, wooden two-story house covered with ivy and surrounded by huge oaks. The nurse carefully guided Louise toward the door and lifted the knocker several times. The door slowly opened, and there stood a woman at least six feet tall. She was dressed all in black. She had thin blue lips. She was fifty or so and very gaunt looking. The nurse pointed out that Dr. Crill had ordered that Louise be admitted.

"Here are the documents," she said.

As Louise entered, the foul air was thick with medicinal and body odors. She heard people moaning, laughing loudly, and screaming. Louise was crying. She sobbed, "Crill has won. I'm in an insane asylum. Oh God, please help me. I will surely die in this place."

"You won't die; it just might be good for you here, young lady," stated the tall woman in black. She was not smiling. "Come with me."

Louise followed her upstairs to a large room filled with cots. There were bars on the four windows. Looking out the windows, she saw only large oaks and a patch of grass below.

"This is your bed, number eighty-seven." It was a bare mattress covered with urine stains on a worn-out set of springs.

Louise was pale with shock. "Where are the sheets, covers, and a pillow?"

"They're being washed," the lady in black said coldly. "Miss Gains expired last night; she had the croup."

I feel like I am going insane, Louise thought.

The lady in black forced her to sit on the bed by grasping her shoulders and pushing her firmly down. The lady then smiled triumphantly.

"You missed supper. You have to wait for breakfast. The toilet is at the end of the hall. You have to wait your turn. Your bedding should be here soon. Don't make trouble, miss," she said, scowling at Louise.

"I'm not a *miss*; my husband is Dr. John Lunt. He will get me out of this nightmare."

"We'll see about that. You have been admitted by Dr. Crill from Boston General Hospital. You have been diagnosed as a paranoid schizophrenic. He is not likely to change his mind. You are here under my charge; get used to it."

Louise thought, *She is like a cruel guard in a prison. Wait in line to use the toilet? There must be thirty people on this floor.* Louise began to sob again. She walked to one of the windows. The sun was setting. *I know John's clinic is not far from here. Those great oaks out there are the same ones near the clinic.* She put her hand on the window and could feel the temperature rapidly dropping. She saw the great oaks near the asylum begin to stir in the wind, and ice formed on the branches and the trunks. The wind increased. She could hear the tortured limbs as ice covered them and turned them black. The wind and the ice worked too well together. The sound of their torture became unbearable. She vaguely remembered the large oak near the iron door where she'd entered the asylum.

Her roommates began to panic. Some of the women ran up and down the middle of the dorm, screaming, "We are going to die!" The windows began to rattle. There was also much commotion on the men's floor below.

"I've got to get out of here." Louise headed toward the stairs. She'd thought the stairway was clear, but some of the men were right ahead of her on the staircase. The wind increased dramatically. The sound of the huge, tortured oaks became louder. Just as they reached the foyer, a great tree fell on the front of the asylum. Suddenly the whole entrance was open, smashed by the nearby oak. Louise and the men didn't hesitate. They rushed out the door together. She was dressed only in a course nightshirt. She had no shoes. The men who followed her were also in their nightclothes. She was terrified. The oaks, heavy with black ice, were disintegrating and falling to the forest floor. She looked up to see the limbs cracking and falling and ran erratically to get out of the way. Her bare feet began to turn numb, but she kept running.

"The clinic—I see the light. Oh God, help me to get to John. I can't feel my feet. I am so cold."

She shook as the cold wind seemed to go right through her nightshirt. She was sure that horrible woman in black was right behind her. She at last saw John's addition to the clinic.

"God, please let him be there. I don't want to die out here."

John was very depressed. He sat in his chair, peering out the picture window at the sea and the oaks. He didn't know his Louise was in that terrible asylum so close he could walk to it. He stared at those old oaks, naked and dark. Churning black clouds were forming to the east. The oaks began to stir. John could see the effect of the wind on the ocean, which seemed to be moving swiftly toward the cliffs and the clinic. Soon the ice storm appeared. The oaks began to glisten. The ever-increasing wind moved the limbs, and even the trunks twisted slightly. They moved as the wind tortured them. The oaks, deeply covered with ice, began to shatter loudly like cracks of thunder.

Suddenly most of his picture window became frosted. Up in the left part of the window, a scene began to form within the frost. He was sure it was the park in Japan. Louise appeared in her beautiful white dress. She was on the little bridge that spanned the brook. She was happy and smiling. The storm raged; great limbs were falling and thundering to the ground. John noticed the tortured sounds of the big oak nearby that hung partly over his office. The image of Louise was still etched in the frost. Suddenly he looked to the lower right side of the window; there was a terrified face, and it was looking up. The tortured tree appeared as if it were about to fall. John rushed out the door. He immediately looked at the place where the figure must have been standing.

It was cold, and ice covered the grass, yet he could see faint signs of footprints. They were fresh. About fifteen yards away, he saw a form dressed in what appeared to be rags. It was Louise. She was moaning. She whispered his name and passed out. He picked her up. Jacque appeared, looking terrified. "Is she?"

"No, but we must get in the house. Carry her, Jacque, and follow me." John found a little-known cellar door close by. They plunged in and quickly found their way to the main floor.

Soon John and Louise were curled up by the fire that Jacque had built. Jacque also brought in blankets. She was awake and smiling. "John, God was there. A huge oak fell on the asylum, and the door—that iron door—opened, and I got out. Many got out. Poor souls."

In a short while John's Dad arrived from town. He rushed in and put his arms around Louise. John knew that she would be safe.

"Dad, see that she stays warm. Jacque, come with me." They took the rig directly into the oaks. The wind was still howling, but most of the damage was done. The asylum was destroyed. The ice and the surrounding oaks had done their terrible work. Soon Jacque spotted ice-covered lumps. They were people—inmates from the asylum. Both men picked them up and put them in the wagon. They found five. They rushed them back to the house. Jacque, John, and his dad got them inside and put them by the fire. After the inmates had taken hot baths, John and his father found clothes and blankets for them. Later, a great meal was prepared for all of them, and finally they were put in rooms with more warm blankets and soft beds.

John, with much emotion, exclaimed, "Jacque, Dad, these men are not insane. They are only developmentally disabled. That's a misdiagnosis all too common. We must help them. They are still young and strong. Let's check with the pastors. Maybe some kind families would take them in."

Later, Pastor Ronald Keith, a prominent minister in the area, met with John.

"Pastor Keith, have you heard about the destruction of the asylum?"

"Yes, John, what a wretched place. I'm glad it is gone. There are no plans to restore it or build another. It is a miracle. Apparently, shortly after you and Jacque rescued the men in the snow, concerned hospital people looking for Louise found the rest of the men and women hiding in a shed near the asylum. They took them to the hospital. They are doing well."

"Pastor, we took in five men who were patients. They need help. These are good men, just a little slow mentally. They just need a good Christian family to love them and let them be a part of their home."

"John, you are right—as long as they are gentle and want to be a part of a family. These good people are mostly farmers out here, and some are seaman. The men will probably have to work."

"That is fine, Pastor. Will you help?"

"Yes, John. I have some families in mind."

"Thanks. Pastor. Keep me informed as to their progress."

"Don't worry, John; God knows about them and will guide us in this endeavor."

When John arrived back to the house, Louise was waiting in the warm kitchen, looking somewhat sad. "These men do not want to leave, poor souls. They feel safe, and they like it here."

"I am sure. Considering what they had to live with, I don't blame them. I just paid a visit to Pastor Keith, a good and capable man. He has agreed to try to find them homes where they will be happy and be able to contribute to society."

"I see. Well, John, that is wonderful. What are we going to do in the future? That Dr. Crill has won. You cannot practice medicine in this area, especially in this house."

"I know, Louise; I am still trying to figure it out. We don't have to do anything. You know, we have the shipping business."

"That is not what you are about, John. You are not a quitter."

"You're right, but where does this hatred for progress end? Wherever we go, it will end the same way. There are Dr. Crills everywhere, and I'm sick of their jealousy, hatred, and stupidity."

"You are right, John. They nearly killed me, but that doesn't mean we have the right to give up. What's that noise? It sounds like men talking just outside our front entrance."

Jacque opened the door. In unison, at least thirty men wearing winter coats over their white uniforms asked, "Is Louise home?"

Jacque laughed. "You people are from Boston General Hospital, aren't you?"

"Yes, is Dr. John here?" one of them blurted.

At that moment, John and Louise appeared.

All thirty men sang loudly, "For he's a jolly good fellow!"

John and Louise were moved. These men made up the bulk of the hospital staff. "We want you to understand that we know what Crill has done to you.

We are sorry. Until Crill is fired, we will not return to work. He is mean, and many of us think he is mentally imbalanced. You didn't know, I'm sure, that over two hundred of your patients gathered in front of the hospital last night and demanded that Crill be punished and said that they would not be treated by anyone from the hospital or any other clinic surrounding the hospital. They had Crill Must Go signs. They loudly chanted, 'Louise, Louise, Louise.' Most of the staff joined in the chant. Crill was beside himself. He loudly swore to get them all. The sheriff came and led him off. We were told it was for his own protection."

Within a month, John and his dad were asked to come to the hospital to meet the new administrator. He was a very distinguished MD and a former classmate of John's. Dr. Fredricks knew all about John's Asian medicine expertise and the following he and his father had developed. He wanted to know if there was some way the hospital could work with John and his father.

Later that evening, Louise turned to John and smiled. They appreciated the invitation Dr. Fredricks had offered. "We must go on. The world needs you, John," Louise whispered.

John took her in his arms and led her to his office, and together they gazed into their future through the frosty window.

Printed in the United States
By Bookmasters